DARK HUNTER

THE WOODEN SKULL

D1535141

Bloomsbury Education
An imprint of Bloomsbury Publishing Plc

50 Bedford Square
London
WC1B 3DP
UK

1385 Broadway
New York
NY 10018
USA

www.bloomsbury.com

First published 2015

British Library Cataloguing-in-Publication Data
A catalogue record for this book is available from the British Library.

ISBN
PB: 978-1-4729-0831-5
ePub: 978-1-4729-0832-2
ePDF: 978-1-4729-0833-9
XML: 978-1-4729-2790-3

Library of Congress Cataloging-in-Publication Data
A catalog record for this book is available from the Library of Congress.

10 9 8 7 6 5 4 3 2 1

Typeset by Newgen Knowledge Works (P) Ltd., Chennai, India
Printed and bound by CPI Group (UK) Ltd, Croydon CR0 4YY

This book is produced using paper that is made from wood
grown in managed, sustainable forests. It is natural, renewable and
recyclable. The logging and manufacturing processes conform to the
environmental regulations of the country of origin.

recommended by

www.catchup.org

Catch Up is a not-for-profit charity
which aims to address the problem of
underachievement that has its roots in
literacy and numeracy difficulties.

DARK HUNTER

THE WOODEN SKULL

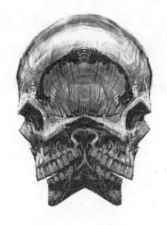

BENJAMIN HULME-CROSS
ILLUSTRATED BY NELSON EVERGREEN

A & C BLACK
AN IMPRINT OF BLOOMSBURY
LONDON NEW DELHI NEW YORK SYDNEY

The Dark Hunter

Mr Daniel Blood is the Dark Hunter.
People call him to fight evil demons,
vampires and ghosts.

Edgar and Mary help Mr Blood
with his work.

The three hunters need to be strong and
clever to survive…

Contents

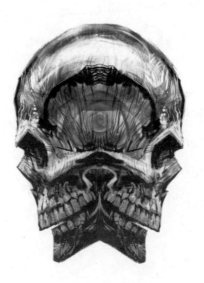

Chapter 1

The Bridge

Mr Blood, Mary and Edgar were standing near a bridge in the town of Blackwell. The river water was dirty and full of all the town's rubbish.

"I am going back to the inn to sit by the fire," Mr Blood said. "Come back inside when you are ready." He walked away.

Mary saw two men on the bridge. There was something strange about them.

"Look, Edgar!" said Mary, "those two men over there on the bridge. They..."

"They look **exactly** the same," Edgar said, "how strange!"

The two men looked like twins. They were just the same as each other in every way.

The men had the same face, the same haircut. Even their clothes were a perfect match. They stood looking at each other in the middle of the bridge.

Edgar could see one difference between the men, however. One man looked very ill and very unhappy. The other man had a nasty smile.

The men stood there saying nothing.
Then, as Edgar watched, he saw that
bit-by-bit the unhappy man's face changed.
He stopped looking sad. Soon he looked
quite calm and happy.

That man stepped up onto the low wall at the side of the bridge. The other man did the same. Then, without a word, the two men jumped off the bridge.

Mary and Edgar cried out and ran onto the bridge. As they ran they both saw a small object rolling towards them. One of the men had dropped it before he jumped. Mary stopped to pick it up.

Edgar kept on running until he reached the wall of the bridge. He leaned over.

The men had vanished in the dirty river.

By the time Mary got to the wall of the bridge a few other people were also looking down into the dirty river.

"Another jumper!" one lady said. "We won't be seeing him again. The currents are strong and they suck you under."

"There were two of them," said Edgar. But nobody heard him. The people who had stopped were walking away.

"That was horrible!" Edgar said to Mary. "What was that thing they dropped?"

"Thing? What thing?" Mary snapped. She sounded very angry. Edgar didn't know why.

"The thing that fell," Edgar said. "You picked it up."

He could see it in her hand. He grabbed it. It was a small wooden carving of a skull with two faces.

"It's mine!" Mary grabbed the skull back. "Why can't you just leave me alone?"

She turned and ran back towards the inn where they were staying.

Edgar stared after her. He didn't understand.

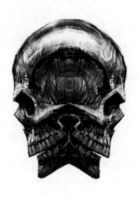

Chapter 2

The Inn

By the time Edgar got back to the inn, Mary had locked herself in her room.

"Open the door," demanded Edgar. "We need to talk."

"Leave me alone," shouted Mary.

Edgar tried to find Mr Blood. He wanted Mr Blood to talk to Mary but Mr Blood had gone out.

Edgar went to his room and sat on his bed. He kept thinking about the two men on the bridge. Were they twins? Why did they jump? One of them had looked sad, but the other seemed to be happy. So why had he jumped to his death?

Edgar tried to talk to Mary again a few times that evening. Each time, she told him to go away. Edgar did not know what was the matter with Mary but he knew that something was very wrong.

It was getting late and Mr Blood had
not come back. Edgar decided to go to bed.
He hoped that Mary would be better in the
morning.

In the middle of the night, Edgar woke
up. He could hear terrible howling. He got
up and walked along the hall.

The howling grew louder. It seemed to be coming from Mary's room. He knocked at the door, but the howling carried on.

Mr Blood came out from his room and the landlord and landlady of the inn came to see what all the noise was about. They unlocked Mary's door.

They found Mary curled up on the floor next to her bed.

Mary was holding something in her hand and howling. Her eyes rolled. Her face was white and her hair damp. She seemed to have a bad fever.

They lifted Mary back onto her bed. The landlady washed Mary's face with warm water. After a while, Mary stopped howling and went to sleep.

There was a tall mirror in the corner of the room. As Edgar turned to leave he looked in the mirror and got a shock. He saw that Mary was staring straight at him.

He gave a cry and turned back to the bed. But Mary's eyes were closed and she was asleep.

"She just opened her eyes," Edgar said.

"I don't think so," said the landlady. "Don't worry, people do funny things when they have a fever."

The landlady offered to stay up and watch Mary for the night. Mr Blood thanked her, and told Edgar to go back to bed.

Edgar went back to his room but he couldn't sleep. There were too many strange thoughts in his head. Mary's sudden fever. The way she had seemed to stare at him. The wooden skull. The jumping men...

Chapter 3

The Search

It was almost dawn before Edgar fell asleep. But he didn't rest for long. Again he was woken by the sound of someone crying out. He ran to Mary's room.

Mr Blood was there. The landlady was sitting on the floor, holding a hand to her head.

"She's gone," the woman gasped, pointing at the open window. "She hit me and climbed out."

Mr Blood dashed across the room and leaned out of the window. "We must find her," he shouted to Edgar. They raced down the stairs and out into the street. There was no sign of Mary.

Edgar looked back up at her window.

"Look!" he shouted. Mr Blood looked up just in time. They both saw Mary climbing back in through the window.

They ran back upstairs and into Mary's room. She was sitting up in bed, smiling. She looked well and happy.

"Mary!" cried Mr Blood. "What were you thinking? That woman was helping you and you hit her."

"Did I?" Mary asked. "I didn't mean to. I feel so tired. Let me sleep a little longer." She lay back down in the bed and closed her eyes.

"Something's not right," Edgar said to Mr Blood, as they left the room and went down the stairs.

"You'll have to find somewhere else to stay, sir," said the landlord. "That girl hurt my wife."

"Mary is sick," Mr Blood snapped. Then he turned to the landlady. "Tell me what happened. Mary does not hurt people without good reason."

"She was holding something in her hand," said the woman. "It looked like a wooden charm. She was squeezing it so tight I thought she would hurt her hand."

"What happened next?" asked Mr Blood.

"I reached out to take the charm and just then she woke up," said the landlady. "Mary sat up in bed. She had a big smile on her face. And then she hit me over the head and climbed out of the window."

"What sort of wooden charm?" asked Mr Blood.

Edgar knew the answer. He told them about what had happened the day before. When he got to the part about the wooden skull Mr Blood turned pale.

"The double skull!" he shouted. "Follow me. Mary is in very great danger!"

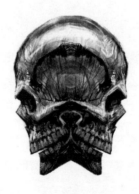

Chapter 4

The Double

Edgar ran upstairs after Mr Blood.

Mary's room was empty once more.

"What is the danger of the double skull?" asked Edgar.

"The double skull is evil," said Mr Blood. "If you take hold of it, then it takes hold of you. First it controls your actions. Next it creates your double – an evil version of yourself. Then it destroys you."

"I think that Mary is being controlled by the double skull. Or we may even have seen her double."

"Do you think the two men who jumped from the bridge were a man and his double?" asked Edgar, "and the double made the man jump?"

Mr Blood nodded grimly.

Edgar felt sick. "How do we stop it?" he said, "we have to help Mary!"

"Destroy the skull and we destroy the double," said Mr Blood. "Hurry, we have to get to the bridge."

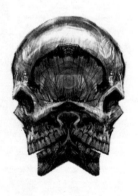

They ran out of the inn and towards the river, shouting Mary's name. People stopped and stared at them as they raced along the road. Up ahead they could see the bridge.

And then they saw Mary. She was walking onto the bridge.

"Mary!" cried Edgar. "Don't do it!"

She turned and smiled at him. He saw another Mary standing on the bridge. This Mary looked very tired and sad.

"That's the real Mary!" Mr Blood shouted. "The girl nearer us is the double. I'll deal with her. You get to the real Mary. Get that skull away from her and destroy it." Mr Blood took a knife from his belt and raced towards the double.

Edgar ran past the false Mary and onto the bridge. The real Mary didn't seem to see him as he came close to her.

"Mary, give me the skull," Edgar begged. Mary didn't answer. She was staring back along the bridge.

She looked tired and ill. But as Edgar watched, her face began to change. The colour came back to her cheeks and she smiled. She seemed happy and calm.

Then Edgar remembered that the man on the bridge had done the same thing just before he jumped.

Behind Mary, Edgar saw a cart coming from the other side of the bridge. It was pulled by two horses. Edgar looked behind him. The double was walking forward, towards the real Mary. There was no sign of Mr Blood.

The double stepped up onto the wall at the side of the bridge. The real Mary did the same.

"Mary! No!" Edgar cried.

Edgar ran towards the real Mary. He grabbed at the skull that she held in her hand, and snatched it away from her, pulling her off the wall and onto the bridge. Mary lashed out at him and scratched his face with her nails. The double screamed and sprang at Edgar.

As the cart passed them, Edgar threw the double skull under its wheels.

The horses reared up wild with terror. The skull cracked as the cart ran over it.

The fake Mary howled and stumbled sideways, to the edge of the bridge. Then she tripped and toppled over the wall. With one final scream, Mary's double fell into the dark river.

Mr Blood came limping onto the brid
and Edgar ran over to help Mary. Her ey
flickered and opened. She stared up at him.

"Edgar, how did you get those scratches
on your face?" she asked.